"My wish is that every child in the world
will know the magic of Christmas."

Holly Claus
The Christmas Princess

BRITTNEY RYAN

Illustrated by LAUREL LONG with JEFFREY K. BEDRICK

HarperCollins*Publishers*

For Robert . . . and John, Diane, and Emma. I love you.
—B.R.

For Anja . . . with love.
—J.K.B.

Holly Claus: The Christmas Princess
Text and illustrations copyright © 2007 by Brittney Ryan

Printed in the U.S.A.

Library of Congress Cataloging-in-Publication Data
Ryan, Brittney.
  Holly Claus : the Christmas princess / by Brittney Ryan ; illustrated by Laurel Long with Jeffrey
K. Bedrick. — 1st ed.
    p.   cm. — (Julie Andrews collection)
  Summary: Santa Claus's daughter, Holly, comes to Earth seeking an end to the curse cast upon
her and the Land of the Immortals by an evil wizard, whose own punishment will end only if Holly
willingly gives him her pure heart.
  ISBN 978-0-06-144022-9 (trade bdg. : alk. paper)
  ISBN 978-0-06-144023-6 (lib. bdg. : alk. paper)
  1. Fairy tales. [1. Fairy tales. 2. Princesses—Fiction. 3. Santa Claus—Fiction. 4. Magic—Fiction.
5. Wizards—Fiction.] I. Long, Laurel, ill. II. Bedrick, Jeffrey K., ill. III. Title.
PZ8.R899Hol 2007   2007018372
[Fic]—dc22   CIP
                                                                                          AC

Typography by Jeanne L. Hogle
1 2 3 4 5 6 7 8 9 10
❖
First Edition

Forever is a kingdom far away, where magical and mythical creatures mingle with real-life heroes whose acts of generosity and compassion live on after their earthly lives have ended. Ringed with glittering glaciers, Forever can sometimes be seen in the icy regions of our world. Here griffins, fairies, and fauns live alongside immortal heroes, artists, champions, and great thinkers, all of whom continue their lives' work in the Kingdom of Forever. And here, of course, lives the King of Forever—the most generous soul of all: Nicholas Claus, also known as Santa Claus.

ne December night in 1878, a boy named Christopher was writing a letter to Santa Claus. Santa Claus receives thousands and thousands of letters at Christmas, but Christopher's letter was the one that changed history.

Dear Santa Claus,

You know I have never written. I could never think of anything I needed or wanted for Christmas. But this year, I had a different idea. What do you wish for Christmas, Santa? You always answer children's wishes, but what about your own? Is there one thing in the world that you wish for but do not have? If you will post a letter back to me, I will do all I can to bring your dream to life.

Respectfully, your friend,
Christopher W. C.

In Forever, King Nicholas, also known as Santa Claus, was reading his letters. Tears were falling down his cheeks, and his wife, Queen Viviana, wrapped her arms around him.

He was reading Christopher's letter.

"No one—" Nicholas cleared his throat. "No one has ever asked me what I wish for."

"Do you have a wish?" asked Viviana.

"I wish for a child!" Nicholas knew it was the one thing he dreamed of but did not have.

His wish was granted. King Nicholas made an announcement to the magical inhabitants of Forever:

"My people! This is a great day in our land, for Queen Viviana and I have been blessed with a baby daughter—the first child ever to be born in the Land of the Immortals! You have a princess, my friends, and her name is Holly Claus."

Holly was a beautiful little girl, filled with love. It was said that she had the purest and most compassionate heart of anyone ever born.

Far away, in another world, there lived an evil warlock named Herrikhan who had once lived in Forever. Because of his acts of cruelty, he had been banished from the Land of the Immortals and cursed with a painful band around his head and the loss of his powers. The curse could be broken only if he were to be loved by a pure heart that would be freely given to him.

On the day of Holly's christening, her godmother gave her a magic locket. The locket would protect Holly from harm and remind her of the power of love.

That same day, Herrikhan invaded Forever. Using his wicked powers, he encased Holly's heart with ice—forcing her to live only in a frosty world lest her heart should melt. Herrikhan foretold a terrible future for Holly: She would be free only if she were to marry Herrikhan when she was old enough to do so.

Because of Herrikhan's curse, the Gates of Forever were locked and its inhabitants imprisoned. Santa Claus could no longer travel to the human world, and the wonder of Christmas disappeared altogether.

olly grew up in Forever, but she was often lonely without human friends to play with. She had a circle of animal companions: Tundra, the wolf, her loyal guardian; Empy, the funny penguin; Euphemia, the wise owl; and Lexy, the mischievous fox.

Despite their company, Holly was often sad. "Papa," she said one day, "I know the truth. It is because of me that the Gates of Forever are locked and you cannot bring Christmas magic to the world. If only I could do something to lift the curse!"

Nicholas reassured her by saying, "My beloved daughter, you are the joy of my life. You must know you are not to blame for our circumstances. I believe we will somehow find a way to break the spell and bring Christmas joy back to children everywhere."

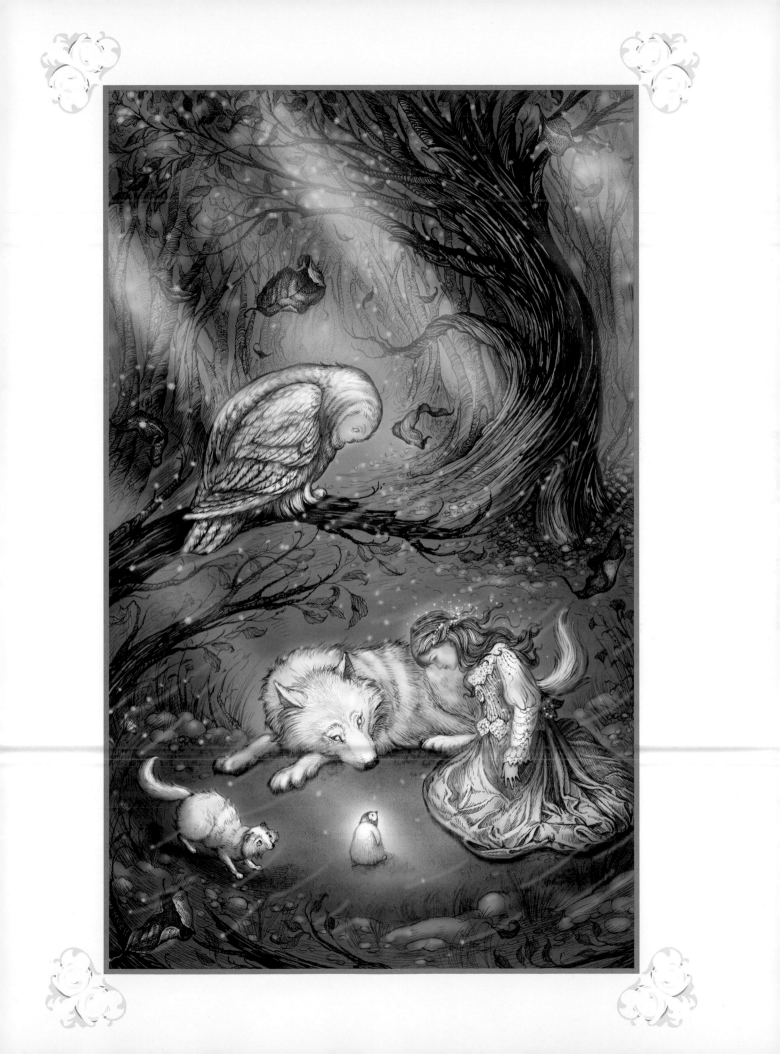

ne evening Holly discovered a splendid treasure sitting atop a grand pedestal in her father's library—the most magnificent book she had ever seen, The Book of Forever. Every inhabitant of the land had a special page describing the accomplishment or good deed that had earned their immortality.

Holly found a page with her own name on it, beautifully inscribed—but below it nothing was written.

"But why is my page blank?" she asked her father.

"It will be filled in time," he reassured her.

"How?" inquired Holly.

"One day you will perform a unique act of kindness for the people of the world, and your generosity will be recorded here," Nicholas replied. "It is your life's purpose, and it will be made clear to you when the moment is right."

Holly wondered how she could perform this special act if she could never leave Forever.

In her room Holly had a magical telescope that showed her all the wonders of the mortal world. She loved to look at the beauty of the oceans and the bustle of the cities, and she longed to visit them someday. But she also saw a world without Christmas—a world where children's dreams and wishes went unanswered. In one place, called the Empire City, Holly could see helpless orphans wandering through the bitterly cold streets, and she began to dream of bringing them all happiness.

olly found herself thinking more and more about the Empire City. She felt drawn to it by a force she did not understand yet could not ignore. Might her life's purpose, the one that would earn her immortality and fill her page in *The Book of Forever*, be fulfilled there? But how to make the journey?

"It will be made clear to you when the moment is right," her father had said.

Finally, one night before Christmas Eve, Holly awoke to discover the sky glistening with a wondrous rainbow. The radiant arc of color appeared to form a bridge over the Gates of Forever. Instinctively, Holly knew this was her chance.

Although leaving the boundaries of Forever meant risking a meeting with Herrikhan and the possibility of never being able to return, Holly put all fear aside.

Harnessing her own team of reindeer to a sleigh, with their leader, Meteor, at the front and her animal friends at her side, Holly soared across the rainbow bridge to freedom.

They arrived with the dawn. The snowy Empire City stretched out beneath Holly, glowing with light and its own spirit.

Gently, softly, the sleigh landed in Central Park. A ragged band of children was huddled around a small fire, and Holly approached them. She explained that she was new to the city, and one of the orphans, a boy named Jeremy, offered to help her find a job and a place to live.

Jeremy led Holly to Carroll's Curiosities and Wonders, a shop filled with magnificent toys of all kinds. There Holly met kindly Mr. Kleiner, who ran the shop, and its mysterious owner, Mr. Carroll. Mr. Kleiner offered Holly a job in the toy shop. All day long she met an endless stream of children and helped them to find the toys of their dreams.

Just as the rays of the setting sun were glinting through the windows, a tall, dark man appeared in the toy shop. He said his name was Hunter Hartman.

"Perhaps you can help me, miss," said Mr. Hartman. "I have to buy a number of toys—gifts for poor children," he added quickly. Of course, Holly agreed to help him, and together they selected dozens of toys.

nce Mr. Hartman had finished buying the toys, he invited Holly to attend the opera with him. Although there was something about Mr. Hartman that made her uneasy, she agreed to join him that evening.

Holly wore a beautiful gown covered with magic crystals that made a pattern of enchanted lace. Mr. Carroll was at the opera too. Holly saw him watching her, and she felt as if they had known each other forever.

After the performance, Mr. Hartman tried to entice her to remove her locket in exchange for a magnificent necklace of diamonds and pearls. All at once, Holly realized that Mr. Hartman was really Herrikhan in disguise, trying to trick her, and she refused to remove the locket.

olly fled from Mr. Hartman and returned to the toy shop. It was late at night as she walked up the stairs and discovered a richly carved door. Holly gently pushed it open and beheld an amazing sight indeed!

Mr. Carroll was standing on the other side, as if he had been waiting for her. He showed her around his secret workshop. Holly was astonished by the hundreds of toys and inventions that bobbled and buzzed across the floor, through the air, and up the walls.

Mr. Carroll and Holly talked late into the night about the wonder of the toys he had created.

"This reminds me of Santa's workshop in Forever!" she told him.

 strange look came over Mr. Carroll's face. "Don't you believe in Santa Claus?" Holly asked.

"I did when I was a boy," he replied. "I even wrote Santa Claus a letter once, asking what he wished for. And I got an answer!" He laughed and pulled a dusty, unopened letter from his desk to show her. "But I never opened the letter. That was the Christmas my mother went away and I stopped believing in everything."

Suddenly Holly realized who Mr. Carroll was. "*You* are Christopher W. C.," she said. "It was *your* letter that made my father's wish come true. And I am the child he wished for."

Holly told Christopher the truth—the story of her life—everything about the Kingdom of Forever, and Herrikhan and his curse, and Santa Claus, her father. But Christopher did not believe her. It all sounded preposterous to him.

Holly knew that Herrikhan would be back. And because she was in love with Christopher, she worried that Herrikhan might try to hurt him. The only way to ensure his safety would be for her to leave the toy shop altogether.

Taking the locket from around her neck, she gave it to Christopher.

"I know you do not believe me," Holly said. "But promise me you will keep this forever. It will protect you, as it has protected me."

olly left Christopher alone in his workshop. Feeling sad and confused, he opened the letter.

Dear Christopher,
    In your letter, you asked me a question that I had never before been asked. I thought that you should know my wish. It was for a child of my own. Because of your selfless love and willingness to give instead of receive, I have been blessed with a daughter, Princess Holly, and your name will be inscribed in *The Book of Forever*.

Your admirer,
Santa Claus

Christopher Winter Carroll stared at the yellowed paper. He knew now that Holly had been telling the truth. For a moment he stood still. He must find Holly, for he held in his hand the locket, the one thing that would save her! He dashed from the shop.

olly waited for Herrikhan in the park. The weather had turned warm because of a deadly spell that Herrikhan had cast. The snow was melting, and so was Holly's heart. She began to feel weak, and her breathing grew labored.

All at once, Herrikhan appeared before her. "Just say the word and I'll save you," he sneered. "You'll feel neither pain nor sorrow ever again for all eternity."

"Never!" Holly whispered.

"Holly!" a voice shouted. It was Christopher. In that moment, Holly knew how to conquer her enemy: with love.

She turned to the evil warlock. "If you will let Christopher live, I will not only go with you willingly, I will *love* you."

Herrikhan looked at her in amazement. How could she love him after all he had done to cause her misery?

In his own heart, he felt a tiny bit of warmth begin to grow. And with that, his whole being exploded. In moments, the only thing that remained of Herrikhan was a small circle of ashes. The warlock's curse was conquered by Holly's act of love.

Far away in the Kingdom of Forever, the big gates swung open. At last Santa Claus could once again bring the magic of Christmas to the world.

Joining hands, Christopher Winter Carroll and Holly Claus stepped into the sleigh that would take them home.

Inside the king's library, shimmering words began to appear on the page that had always been blank.

Holly Claus, the Christmas Princess, the courageous young woman who followed her heart and saved Christmas with her love.

Holly's story would now be inscribed in The Book of Forever for all time. Now every child in the world would know the magic of Christmas forevermore.

From the Desk of Holly Claus

My story does not end here . . . the magic continues. I
live in the Land of the Immortals, in the Kingdom of
Forever. I would love to hear from you, so please send me
a letter at the following address:

Holly Claus
The Royal Palace
The Kingdom of Forever
The Land of the Immortals 90209-1225

Yours in Enchantment,

Holly Claus™

P.S. Please visit us at www.hollyclaus.com

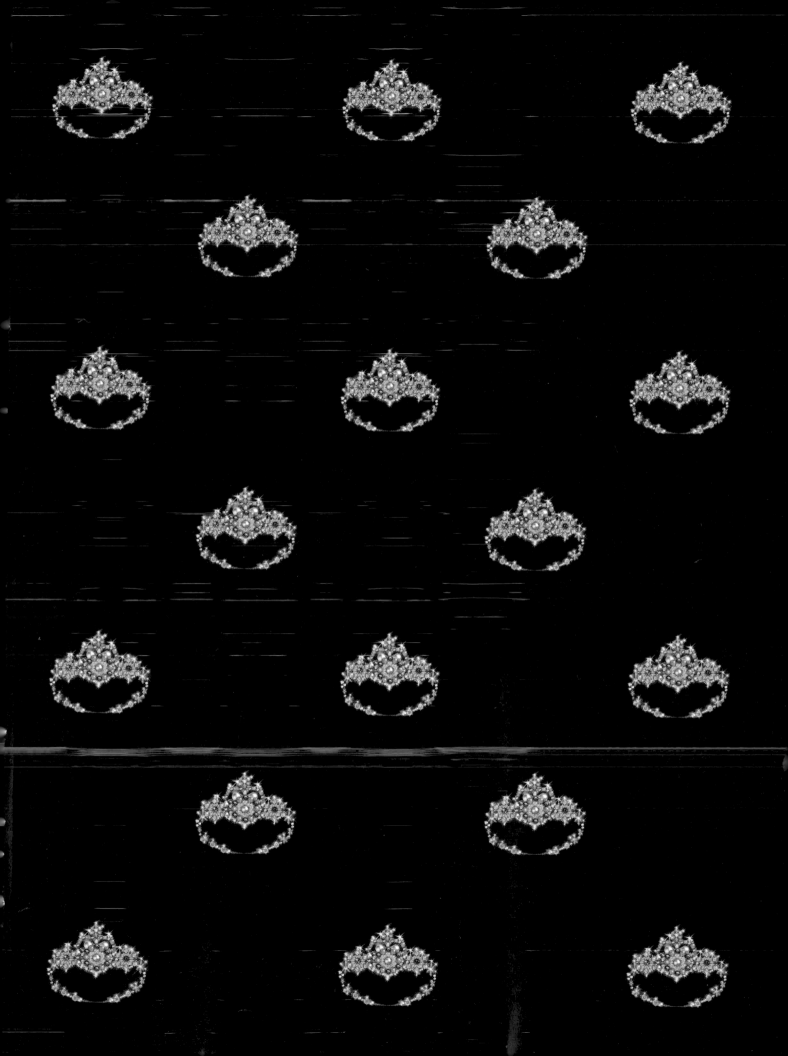